PINK and SAY

Patricia Polacco

Philomel Books

To the memory of Pinkus Aylee

Published simultaneously in Canada. Manufactured in China by South China Printing Co. Ltd.
Book design by Donna Mark. The text is set in Cochin.

Library of Congress Cataloging-in-Publication Data
Polacco, Patricia. Pink and Say / written and illustrated by Patricia Polacco. p. cm.
Summary: Say Curtis describes his meeting with Pinkus Aylee,
a black soldier, during the Civil War, and their capture by Southern troops.
1. United States—History—Civil War, 1861-1865—Juvenile Fiction.
[1. United States—History—Civil War, 1861-1865—Fiction. 2. Friendship—Fiction.]
Title. PZ7.P75186Pk 1994 [E]—dc20 93-36340 CIP AC ISBN 0-399-22671-0

40 39 38

When Sheldon Russell Curtis told this story to his daughter, Rosa, she kept every word in her heart and was to retell it many times over in her long lifetime.

Sheldon had been injured in a fierce battle and was left for dead in a muddy, blood-soaked pasture somewhere in Georgia. He was a mere lad of fifteen. He lay there for two days, by his reckoning, only to slip into unconsciousness and fever. He was rescued from this field by another lad who had also been separated from his company.

I will tell it in his own words as nearly as I can:

I watched the sun edge toward the center of the sky above me. I was hurt real bad. For almost a year I'd been in this man's war. The war between the states. Being just a lad, I was wishin' I was home.

My leg burned and was angry from the lead ball that was lodged in it just above my knee. I felt sleepy and everything would go black. Then I'd wake up again. I wanted to go back to our farm in Ohio and sometimes, when I'd fall into one of them strange sleeps, I'd be there with my Ma, tastin' baking powder biscuits fresh out of her wood stove.

Then I heard a voice. For a moment I thought I was fever-dreamin', but then I felt strong hands touch my brow, splash water in my face.

"Bein' here, boy, means you gotta be dead," the voice said as he gave me a drink from his kit. "Where you hit? 'Cause if it's a belly hit, I gotta leave you here," he said.

I had never seen a man like him so close before. His skin was the color of polished mahogany. He was flyin' Union colors like me. My age, maybe. His voice was soothin' and his help was good.

"Hit in the leg," I told him. "Not bad if it don't go green."

"Can you put weight on it?" he asked as he pulled me to my feet. "We gotta keep movin'. If we stay in one spot, marauders will find us. They're ridin' drag and lookin' for wounded."

Next thing I remember was collapsin' in a heap on the ground and rockin' with the pain in my leg. Everything started to go black. Then I remember him pullin' me up on his back. I heard him say, "Lord have mercy, child. You as bad off as I am. I'll tote ya. I can't rightly leave you here."

I remember being pulled and carried, and stumblin'. I remember hard branches snappin' back in my face and mouths full of dirt as we hit the ground to keep from being seen. I remember sloggin' through streams, haulin' up small bluffs and belly-crawlin' through dry fields. I remember these things in half-sleeplike, but I do remember being carried for a powerful long way.

Then fever must have took me good, 'cause I could feel a cool, sweet-smelling quilt next to my face. Soft, gentle warm hands were strokin' my head with a cool wet rag cloth.

"Look at that mornin' that's comin'," a woman's voice said as she spooned oat porridge into me. "Do your momma know what a beautiful baby boy she has?"

"Where am I? Is this heaven?" I asked.

She tossed her head and laughed. "No child, Pinkus brung you home to me—don't you remember?"

The mahogany child, I thought.

"Both you children been on the run for days, and a miracle of God Almighty brung you both here, yes indeed, child, a miracle."

I remember thinkin', Could this war have been so close to this lad's home? I couldn't imagine havin' a war right in his back yard. I looked over and saw him lookin' out the winderlight.

"Guess you don't remember much," he said. "I'm Pinkus Aylee, fought with the Forty-eighth Colored. Found you after I got lost from my company."

"My name is Sheldon. Sheldon Curtis," I said weakly.

"This is my mother, sweet Moe Moe Bay," he said as she smiled at me.

"Lord, Lord, I never thought I'd see my dear boy again," she said as she hugged him. "I been gittin' along, though, Pinkus. Warm things got left in the big house when the family left. Dry goods, too. The rest I been gittin' from the woods. They's a freshwater spring. Still have some chickens, even got an ole cow out back that still gives."

"Then you have been all alone here?" Pinkus asked his mother. "Where is everybody?"

"Your daddy runned off to fight a month ago. All the hands and their children runned off out of harm's way. But I stayed. I prayed to the Lord every day. My prayers were surely answered 'cause He brought my baby back here to stay," she said as her face beamed. "You ain't never gonna leave your momma again, are you, child?" she said softly.

Pinkus looked troubled and didn't answer.

"I'm goin' down to the stream and pound these clothes of yours," she said as she readied to leave us. "If you hear marauders comin', git for the root-cellar door. Stay down there 'til they gone. That's what I been doin'."

"Marauders here?" Pinkus said with alarm.

"They've seen there's nothin' here for them, child....Nothin'!"

As soon as she left us, Pinkus sank to my bedside.

"Sheldon, boy," he whispered, "as soon as you heal up we gotta get away from here. We are puttin' Moe Moe Bay in great danger by bein' here. If they come and find that she's been holdin' troopers…" Then his voice trailed off. "We gotta get back to our outfits if we can find 'em."

"You mean back to the war?" I asked.

I must have gone pale as he went on to say, "It's the only way, ain't it?" Then he looked at me. "Sheldon, you alright? You look bothered," he said as he eased me back.

"You can call me Say," I said. "Everybody in my family calls me Say, not Sheldon. I 'spect you're my family now."

"Near 'nuff, Say. Near 'nuff," he said as he chucked the blanket under my feet. "You can call me Pink," he said softly as he smiled.

For the next week Moe Moe Bay fed us both up good. Raw milk and corn bread never tasted so good in all my born days. It were the first time in months my vittles didn't have any mealy worms in it. She saw to it that I tried to walk a little every day. "So's that mean-lookin' leg don't go stiff on you and cripple up," she'd say.

This place wasn't that much different from our farmhouse in Ohio, more poor maybe, but it smelled the same. Like pine boards and good cookin'. A mess-o'-beans with salt pork, corn bread, greens and onions. When we slept, she sat near us, stoked the fire and watched over us. Never thought I'd feel safe enough to sleep deep again.

"My mother and Kaylo, my father, jumped the broom on this very spot," Pink said as he walked me on my first day outdoors. "And that there was the Master's house. Master Aylee." Pink spoke quietly as he helped me along.

"How come you have his last name?" I asked.

"Boy, when you owned, you ain't got no name of your own. Even Kaylo had to take that name."

As we rested under the willow tree, Pink asked me about my family back home.

"Got one brother still at home to help run the place fer Pa," I answered.

"What was your outfit again?" Pink asked. He'd asked me before.

"Ohio Twenty-fourth. I carried the staff. Wasn't supposed to carry a gun, but then so many died, even us boys had to carry after so many were slaughtered like hogs."

"Least you got to carry. In the Forty-eighth, we couldn't have guns at first. We fought with sticks and hammers and sledges. Can you imagine not trustin' us with our own fight?"

I couldn't imagine such a thing.

"Then when they did finally give us muskets, they were from the Mexican-American War. Those muskets jammed and misfired!"

"Then how, in God's name, can you want to go back?" I asked.

"'Cause it's my fight, Say. Ain't it yours, too? If we don't fight, then who will?"

I had no answer for him, but, God forgive me, I didn't want to ever go back to it!

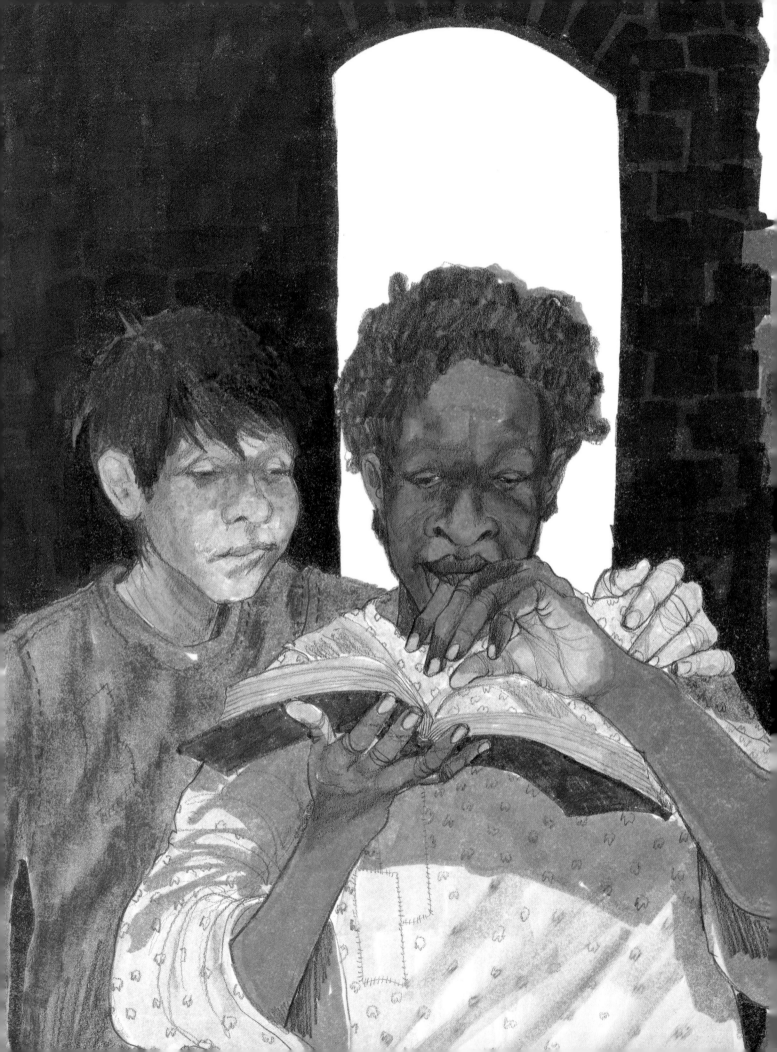

After a few more days I could walk a little steadier but still needed help. Pink took me out by the big house and walked me through it. Weren't much left of it really, it was mostly burned out.

"Master Aylee had a library full of books right here," he said. "He taught me to read, even though it was against the law."

"He must have been a good man," I said.

"More bad than good, Say. Sometimes I think he just liked bein' read to. There was this book of poetry, Say, that was this thick. Every night I'd read out loud to him from that book.

"I blessed this house because of all those beautiful books...but I cursed it, too, for what it stood for."

We walked a bit further.

"To be born a slave is a heap o' trouble, Say. But after Aylee taught me to read, even though he owned my person, I knew that nobody, ever, could really own me."

"You feel hot, Pink," I said. "Lord, I think you are as sick as me. Let me fetch you back to the house."

"I'll be fine, boy. Just a little tired, that's all. I'll be ready to fight, though. I'll be ready to fight."

That night after we ate, Moe Moe Bay came back to the table with a worn old Bible. She was so happy. My heart ached at the thought of tellin' her we'd be leavin' soon.

"Master Aylee showed him how paper talks. Show him, Pink," she said.

He took out a pair of spectacles from his pocket and opened the Bible to the Psalms of David and started to read. His voice was steady and had such wonder. Just hearin' them words made pictures come into my head.

"I surely do wish I could read," I announced to them without thinkin'.

When Pink saw I was ashamed, he took my hand.

"I'll teach you, Say, some one day. I'll teach you."

I could feel my face flushin' up. Then I spoke up. "I done something important," I announced.

"Of course you have, child, of course you have," his mother said.

"I touched Mr. Lincoln's hand. It were near Washington. We were quartered there just before Bull Run. The president himself were shakin' everyone's hands. And I just put my hand right out."

"And he took it?" Pink asked.

"Yep, he took it," I answered.

"Now there's a sign, ain't it?" he said, smilin' broadly.

"Touch my hand, Pink. Now you can say you touched the hand that shook the hand of Abraham Lincoln!"

"Next best thing to touchin' him," Moe Moe Bay said in wonder.

Most of the next day Pink was studyin' an old map. "Marauders don't fan out further than thirty miles or so from their camps. If they come here then their units must be that close. We gotta get south of the river. See here, Say? That's where my troops were headed. We can meet up with them about here, I figure."

"Meet up with who? You ain't leavin'?" His mother's voice caught as she came upon us.

"Now, my mother, you knew we couldn't stay here. You had to know that!" he said as he tried to calm her.

"No, no, my babies…my dear babies!" she cried. She was inconsolable for a time, then she sat still and afeared as she just listened.

"Mother, this war has to be won or this sickness that has taken this land will never stop." Pink always called slavery "the sickness" when we talked. "We have to go." He knelt at her feet.

By the look that came into her eyes, she'd known that this day was comin'.

I could feel my breathin' catch. My chest was heavy. My hands were sweatin' and I felt sick at my stomach. I knew that I had to tell Pink somethin'. I just didn't know how.

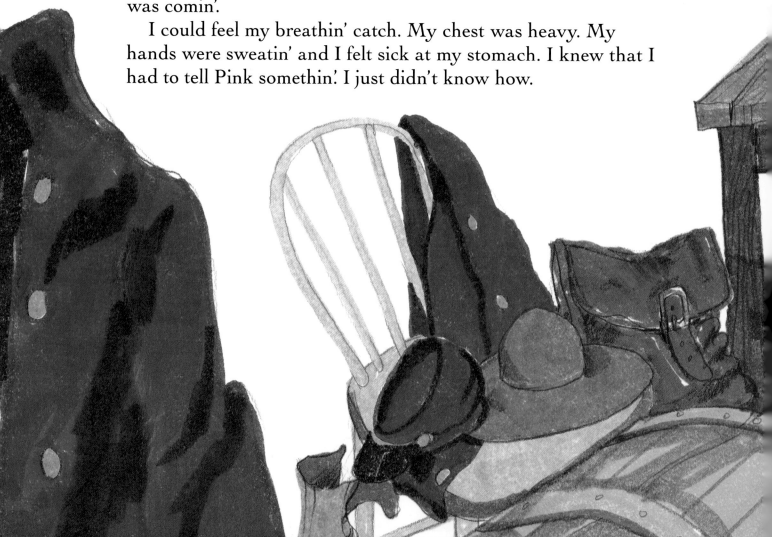

That night I couldn't sleep.

"What's wrong, child?" Moe Moe Bay said from her chair.

"I don't want to go back," I blurted out.

"I know, child," she said. "Of course you don't."

"You don't understand. I took up and run away from my unit. I was hit when I was runnin'." I sobbed so hard my ribs hurt. "I'm a coward and a deserter."

She looked at the fire and said nothing for the longest time. Then her voice covered my cries. "You ain't nothin' of the kind. You a child...a child! Of course you scared. Ain't nobody that ain't."

"I'm not brave like Pink....I'm not brave."

"Child, bein' brave don't mean you ain't afeared. Don't you know that?"

"I don't want to die."

"They's things worse than death, child. But you got nothin' to fear. You are here now, and I'm huggin' you up. You goin' to be an old man someday. When it is your time, the sweet Lord'll send a hummin' bird to fly your soul to heaven. Now, you ain't afeared of hummin' birds, are you?"

Her words brought me sweet sleep. That night I dreamt of hummin' birds and green pastures full of sunlight and wildflowers.

The next mornin' we mustered to leave. We packed corn bread, salt pork and dried beans. I would have done just about anything to stay, but my place was to go with Pink. I owed him that.

Just as we were makin' the last sweep of the place, makin' sure that there were no signs of us ever bein' there, we heard wild screams and shrieks comin' from the woods.

"Marauders!" Pink said as he grabbed a piece of wood for a club.

Moe Moe Bay took it from him. "Git to the root cellar. They ain't got no truck with an old dark woman. You git to that cellar, you hear!"

We didn't like it but then she pushed us. "Hurry, afore they're here!" She lifted the root-cellar door and shoved us in. "Don't come out 'til I tell you!"

We heard the porch steps creak as she ran from the cabin.

"She's drawin' them off," Pink whispered.

When the marauders came in, my heart was poundin' so hard I was sure they could hear it up there above us. There was a terrible commotion as they ransacked, lookin' for food. Then there was silence. A single shot echoed through the trees outside. They let out a war whoop as they thundered off.

We waited for a sign from Moe Moe Bay, but it didn't come. Finally we climbed out and ran outside only to see Moe Moe Bay lyin' just beyond the porch.

"We put you in their way by stayin' here," Pink cried as he rocked her in his arms.

Her eyes were lookin' in a faraway place as he closed them. "Your son loves you, Moe Moe Bay. Your son loves you." He sobbed as he kissed her.

We both held her hand until there was no more warmth in it.

After we buried her under the willow tree, we set out. Pink figured we were a three days' walk from Union troops. He watched the movement of the sun.

Her words still rang in my heart. Her words about bein' brave. My steps were as sure now as they had ever been since the war started. We walked in the open, as clear as a country stroll, until the mornin' of the second day. Then we knew we were bein' followed.

"Take these," Pink said as he took his spectacles from his pocket. "If they catch me with them, there'll be trouble for sure."

When they caught up to us, one yelled at me, "Where you goin' with that darky, boy?"

I was afraid to answer because of my Northern accent. It would, dead sure, give us away.

"Boy, what outfit you part of?" their leader barked.

I couldn't answer.

"You Union, boy?" one jeered as he pulled my uniform from my knapsack.

"No...I ain't no Yankee. I got that from a dead one," I sputtered, trying to convince them.

That was when we were grabbed. My words had given us away.

We were prisoners of the Confederate Army. We were held up in a barn that night. Pink shivered with fever. I held him as he had done for me.

The next mornin' we were thrown into a boxcar. We rode for what seemed two days, stoppin' many times. When the door slid open, the daylight was blindin'. We were loaded into a buckboard and taken through town.

The townsfolk looked hard at us. All they had left for us was mean looks and a heap of hate. We jarred to a stop in front of gates that marked the entrance to a stockade.

"It says Andersonville," Pink whispered.

My heart stopped. I had heard of this place. It was one of the worst of the Confederate camps.

When we were pulled from the buckboard, we fell hard to the ground.

"No, no," I begged as they pulled us both along.

Because of his fever, Pink stumbled and fell. They dragged him along with such meanness. He did not protest until they forced us in different directions.

Then he reached for me and said, "Let me touch the hand that touched Mr. Lincoln, Say, just one last time."

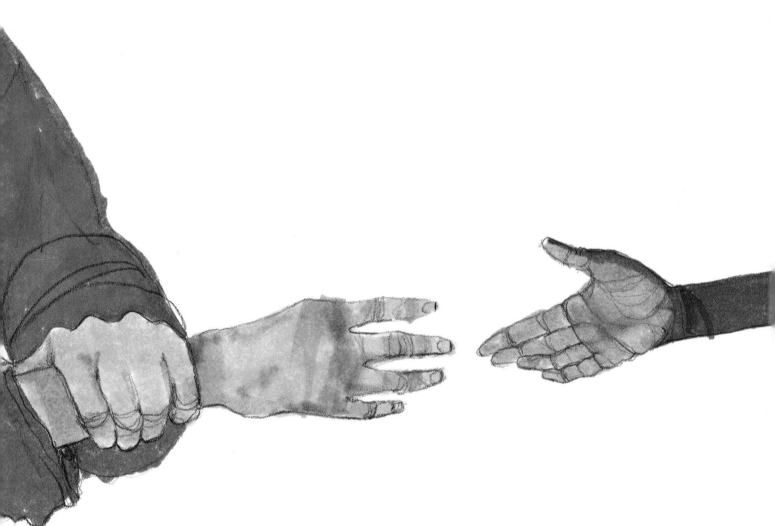

I watched tears fill his eyes and cleaved my hand to his until they wrenched us apart. They smote him and dragged him away from me. He looked back at me and tried to say somethin' more but they crossed his back with knotted hemp and pushed him along.

Sheldon Russell Curtis was released from Andersonville prison some months later, weighing no more than seventy-eight pounds. Andersonville was built to hold only ten thousand prisoners, but by the end of the war it held thirty-three thousand soldiers. There was no fresh water, no shelter and no food. Thirteen thousand men and boys died of starvation and dysentery.

Sheldon Curtis returned to his home and recovered. He settled in Berlin Township in Saranac, Michigan. He married Abagail N. Barnard and fathered seven children. He became a grandfather and a great-grandfather during his long lifetime. He died a very old man in 1924.

Pinkus Aylee never returned home. For him there was to be no wife, no children nor grandchildren to remember him. It was told that he was hanged within hours after he was taken into Andersonville. His body was thrown into a lime pit.

I know this story to be true because Sheldon Russell Curtis told his daughter, Rosa.

Rosa Curtis Stowell told it to her daughter, Estella.

Estella Stowell Barber, in turn, told it to her son, William.

He then told me, his daughter, Patricia.

When my father finished this story he put out his hand and said, "This is the hand, that has touched the hand, that has touched the hand, that shook the hand of Abraham Lincoln."

This book serves as a written memory of Pinkus Aylee since there are no living descendants to do this for him.

When you read this, before you put this book down, say his name out loud and vow to remember him always.